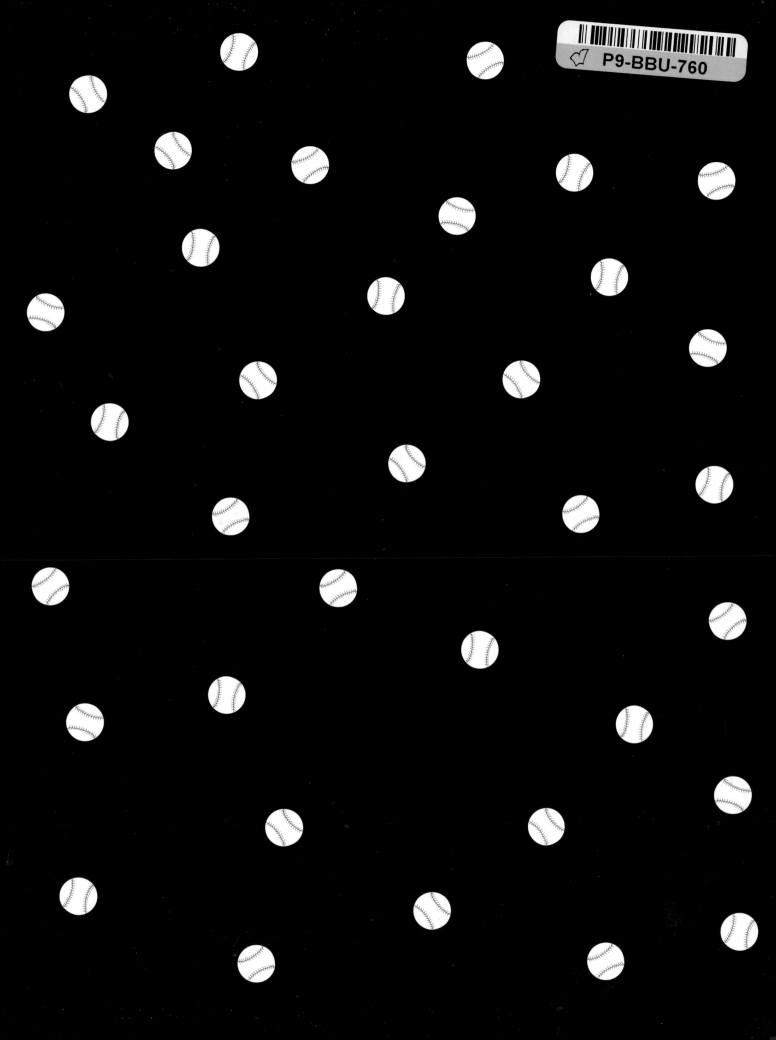

Frankie Goes to Fenway
The Tale of the Faithful, Red Sox–Loving Mouse
Published by:
Three Bean Press, LLC
P.O. Box 15386
Boston, MA 02215
orders@threebeanpress.com • www.threebeanpress.com

Publishers Cataloging-in-Publication Data
Clark, Seneca Teal
Giardi, Sandy
Frankie Goes to Fenway: The Tale of the Faithful, Red Sox–Loving Mouse / by Seneca Clark and Sandy Giardi; illustrated by Julie Decedue.
p. cm.
Summary: Frankie, a Vermont field mouse, moves to Fenway Park and opens a concession stand. When a cat from New York attempts to sabotage the Red Sox, Frankie tries to save the day.
ISBN 0-9767276-3-3
[1. Children—Fiction. 2. Baseball—Fiction. 3. Boston Red Sox—Fiction. 4. Boston—Fiction. 5. Fenway Park—Fiction. 6. New York Yankees—Fiction.] I. Decedue, Julie, Ill. II. Title.
Library of Congress Control Number: 2008925565

Printed in the U.S.A.

FRANKIE GOES TO FENWAY

The Tale of the Faithful, Red Sox-Loving Mouse

Dedicated to baseball fans everywhere

especially:
Chris (Seneca)
Zach, Aurora, William and Nina (Julie)
Mike, Tessa and Beckett (Sandy)

BOS TON

Leaving Vermont

"It's a perfect spring day for the season's home opener against the dreaded Yankees here at Fenway Park," the TV anchor announced. "The Red Sox are at bat. Here comes the pitch.... *Smack*! It's headed for Lansdowne Street! It's out of the park! The Red Sox are off to a fantastic start."

Frankie the field mouse was up on his feet. He could hardly stand the excitement. "That's it! I've got to get to Fenway!"

Frankie was not your average field mouse. While the rest of his family burrowed in their nests, Frankie would sneak to the farmer's window to watch his beloved team play. A loyal fan, the little mouse had never missed a game, and Fenway Park, a field far from his Vermont home, had always called to him.

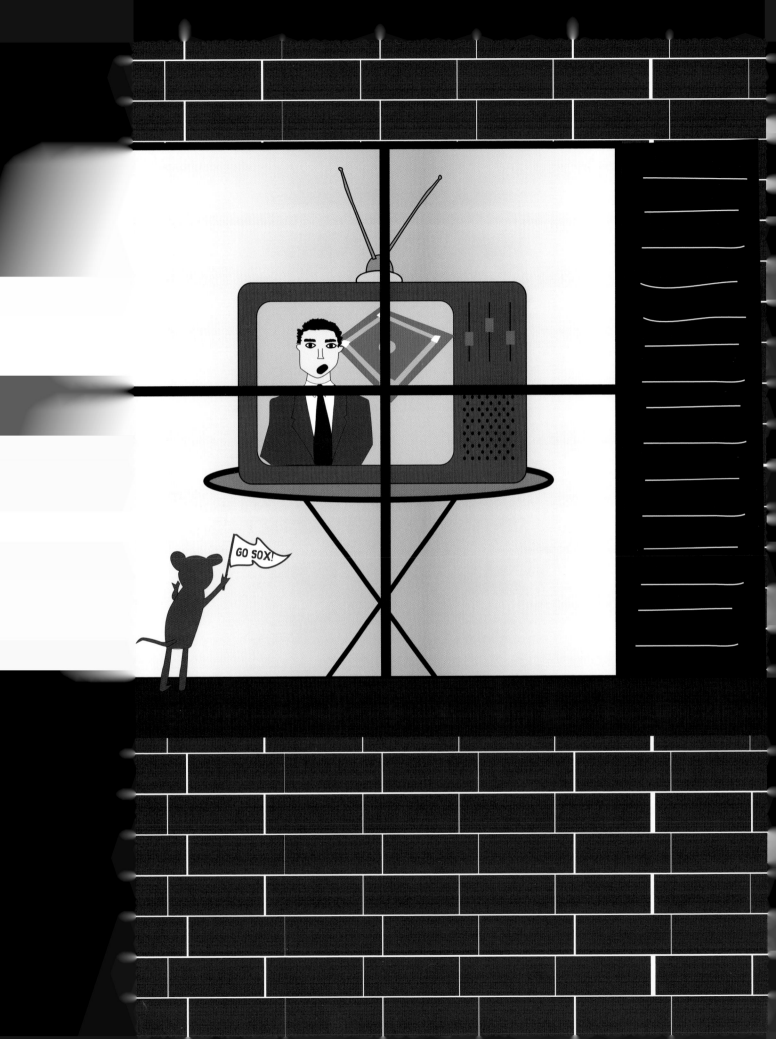

Knowing that the farmer was making a delivery to Boston the next morning, Frankie packed up his things and spent his final night in the starlit countryside, dreaming of what he would see tomorrow.

The next morning, a hopeful Frankie climbed aboard the farmer's truck, and his fellow field mice came to see him off. Though anxious at first, Frankie became more excited with every mile. After a few hours, the truck turned onto a winding stretch along the Charles River. Tall buildings grew up around him, and suddenly the glowing lights of the famous Citgo sign appeared. "I can't believe I'm here!" Frankie squealed. The truck stopped at a red light, and Frankie hopped onto the sidewalk.

Arriving at Fenway

Frankie inched to the curb. Traffic raced toward him. "How am I ever going to cross the street?" he worried. Disheartened for a moment, he heard a voice calling from across the way, "Need tickets?" That was all he had to hear. Frankie mustered up his courage, looked both ways, and darted to the other side.

Tiptoeing through the gates of Fenway Park, Frankie inhaled the scent of sausages cooking and heard the pop, pop, pop of popcorn popping. He scurried through the sea of jersey-wearing fans and dodged the tip of a giant foam finger.

Slipping away from the crowd, Frankie found a hole in the Green Monster, Fenway Park's storied left-field wall. The field stretched out before him. It was spectacular! It was the greenest grass Frankie had ever seen, with crisp, white baselines surrounding the perfect rise of the pitching mound. His heart swelled when he heard "The Star-Spangled Banner," and his spirits soared when the announcer called the players to the field. The game had begun, and Frankie knew he was home.

1 2 3 4

VISITOR

BOSTON

A week passed. Frankie attended every game, cheered for every run and sighed at every out. He had started to make friends with some of the stadium's residents. Legs the spider had lived at Fenway for years. He knew every inch of the park and could point Frankie in eight different directions at once. Bob the pigeon had made a science of scouring the stadium for the finest crumbs. And A-Corn, a thrifty squirrel, was a master at making the morsels he found last.

Life was grand at Fenway, but finding food *was* a problem, especially when the Red Sox were on the road. The animals were forced to snap up cast-off hot dogs and nibbled buns. Frankie hungered for the fresh produce of the farm; there wasn't a chunk of Vermont cheddar cheese to be found. "This is no way to live!" Frankie thought, hurling a stale pretzel to the ground. That's when an idea came to him with the force of a line drive: "I'll open up a concession stand!"

Gourmet Frank's Concession Stand

Gourmet Frank's was a hit! Frankie's friends relished having a choice of delicious new meals. "This is great!" A-Corn exclaimed, cracking open a fresh, salty peanut. "Much better than flies," Legs agreed.

Even Frankie's family and friends back home were excited by his new business since it meant they made regular trips from Vermont to help stock the stand.

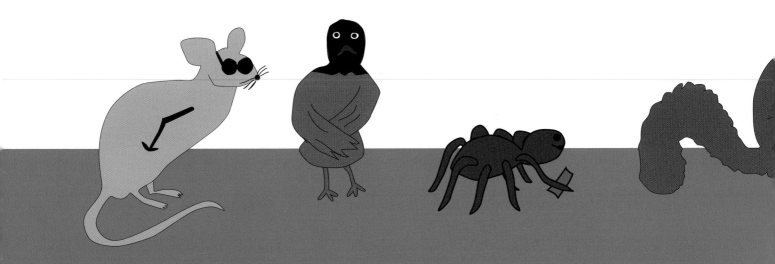

Gourmet FRANK'S

On the menu

hot dogs

sunflower seeds

peanuts

candied bugs

popped acorns

sushi

berries

Cheeses:

Vermont Cheddar

American

Swiss

string

ketchup

As spring turned to summer, the lines at Gourmet Frank's were long and filled with happy customers. Frankie spent his days working the food stand and his nights in the grandstand with his friends. Although he was tired, Frankie had never been happier. His beloved Red Sox were leading the league. They were in first place!

Problems at the Park

But it wasn't long before trouble moved to town....

Slider the cat was from New York City. A Yankees fan through and through, he couldn't believe his family would move to the heart of Red Sox Nation. Slider spent his days exploring Boston with a distaste as strong as stinky blue cheese. The brownstones of Commonwealth Avenue were not nearly as fancy as the buildings of Fifth Avenue, and he missed the steady stream of yellow taxis speeding down the streets.

One day, Slider found himself in Kenmore Square by Fenway Park. "Why not check it out?" he thought. "See what these Red Sox are all about." He slinked past the legs of the ticket collector and made his way inside. A wily cat, Slider could get to places most baseball fans never see. He strutted past the Red Sox locker room and plugged his ears when the organ blared, "Dun, dun, dun, dun...." He hissed at two mice on his way to the bleachers, swatting at one just for fun.

dun, dun, dun, dun

Bleachers →

Slider made his way to the field. The crowd was humming, and he could almost taste the excitement. He had to admit it was easy to get caught up in the fun. A deafening roar made Slider snap out of it.

"Not another grand slam!" moaned the Blue Jay to the Oriole.

"This team is unstoppable!" the Cardinal warbled.

"Are you guys rooting against the home team, too?" Slider asked.

"You bet," the birds chorused.

"Where are you all from?" Slider said, sensing these were new friends.

"Toronto," tweeted the Blue Jay.

"St. Louis," said the Cardinal.

"I'm from Baltimore," the Oriole said. "Are you from around here?"

"No way," Slider sneered. "I'm from the Big Apple!"

"With the way the Red Sox are playing, I bet the Yankees get trounced when they're in town next weekend," taunted the Jay.

"Not if I can help it!" Slider replied. "Are you guys up for a little fun?"

"What do you have in mind?" the birds asked.

"Huddle up," Slider signaled.

5th INNING

Sox vs. Yankees

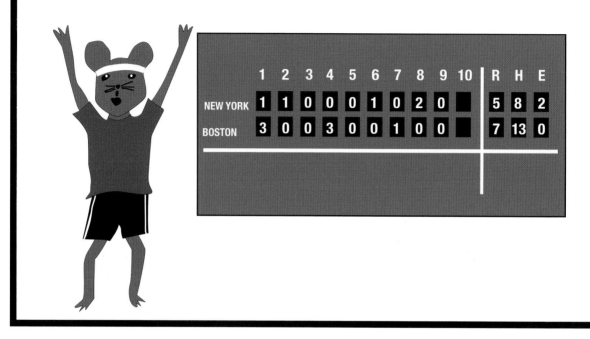

	1	2	3	4	5	6	7	8	9	10	R	H	E
NEW YORK	1	1	0	0	0	1	0	2	0		5	8	2
BOSTON	3	0	0	3	0	0	1	0	0		7	13	0

Frankie was geared up for the Red Sox–Yankees series. The Red Sox were playing so well, they would surely clobber the Yanks. In game one, the Red Sox were victorious. It wasn't by much, but a win was a win. Frankie and his friends breathed a sigh of relief.

	1	2	3	4	5	6	7	8	9	10	R	H	E
NEW YORK	0	0	0	2	2	0	0	0	0	1	5	9	1
BOSTON	0	0	1	0	0	0	1	1	1	0	4	6	2

The next day, Sox fans sat nervously on the edge of their seats. The Pinstripes didn't let up and won in extra innings. Boston's winning streak had ended.

In game three, the Sox were losing badly, and everyone's confidence seemed shaken. On the good plays, the cheers of the crowd weren't as spirited as usual, and the organ couldn't inspire them either. The players were off too, and even the slick-fielding center fielder fumbled catches he would normally make. The Red Sox had lost another game. Disappointed, they headed back to the dugout, while the Yankees celebrated on the diamond. The saddened Fenway faithful looked on.

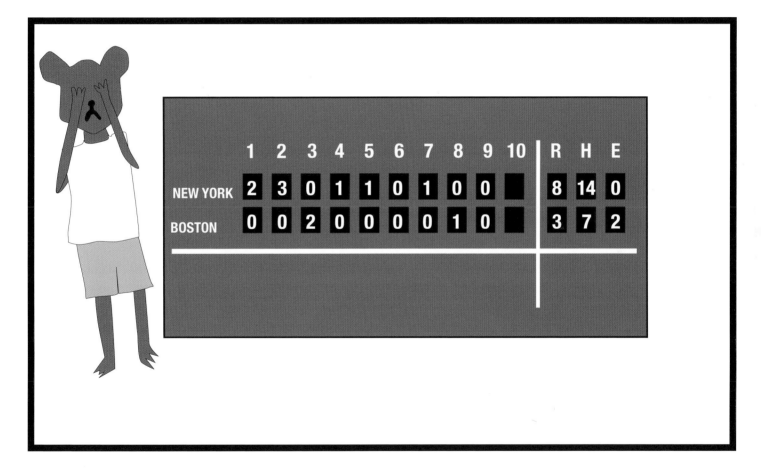

Frankie left his seat with his head hung low. He didn't feel like going back to his stand. Who could eat at a time like this, anyway? As he wandered the concourse, he noticed a streak of gray out of the corner of his eye. "What was that?" Frankie thought. He turned his head and spotted a cat. "What's a cat doing in here? And what's in his mouth? It's our ace pitcher's good luck charm!" Frankie gasped. "No wonder he's been lousy lately!"

Slider's Scheme

Slider spied Frankie as well and noted the look of surprise on his face. "Silly mouse, if I weren't tearing apart this lucky charm, I'd be after you!" he chuckled to himself, gnawing on the trinket. Slider purred, happy with the success of his plan so far. "The birds had better be working on their part of the deal too!"

Indeed they were. The birds were busy in the umpires' room.

"These strings are tough to loosen!" said the Blue Jay, pecking at a baseball.

"I've almost got this one," the Cardinal crowed with a string at the tip of his beak.

"Keep at it, and the stuffing will fly right out of these balls. Even the cleanup hitter won't be able to smack one to Lansdowne Street," chortled the Oriole.

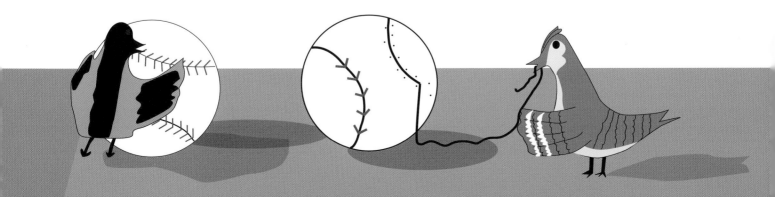

Gourmet FRANK'S

On the menu
hot dogs
sunflower seeds
peanuts
candied bugs
popped acorns
sushi
berries

Cheeses:
Verm
Am
S
S

ketchup

Frankie Frets

Frankie made his way back to his stand. It was nearly dinner-time, and his regulars would be crowding Gourmet Frank's.

"This is crazy, another loss," A-Corn said, nervously pulling on the hairs of his tail.

"I know, the whole team seems off," nodded Bob. "And what's with all of those broken bats? I've never seen so many in one game!"

Legs threw his hands in the air. "They just have to turn things around! There's always tomorrow."

"I'm sure the Sox can pull it off," said A-Corn. "We have to believe!"

"You're right, I need to start thinking positively," Frankie said as the gang began to head home. Then he quickly remembered to warn his buddies, "By the way, I saw a cat in the stadium today, and he looks menacing."

"He *is* mean, look what he did to me," squeaked a hobbling mouse.

"I have a bad feeling about that cat," Frankie confided, shaking his head.

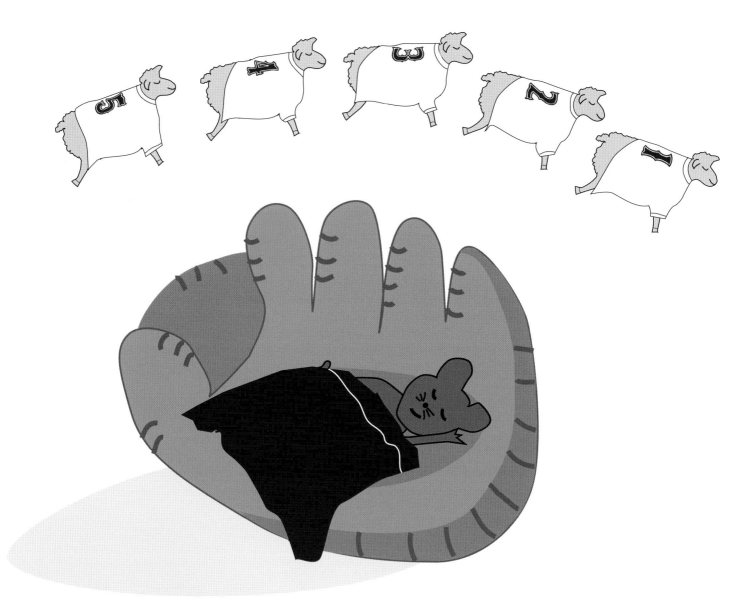

Night settled over Fenway, and the park was nearly empty. Frankie nestled in his glove and counted sheep while trying to sleep.

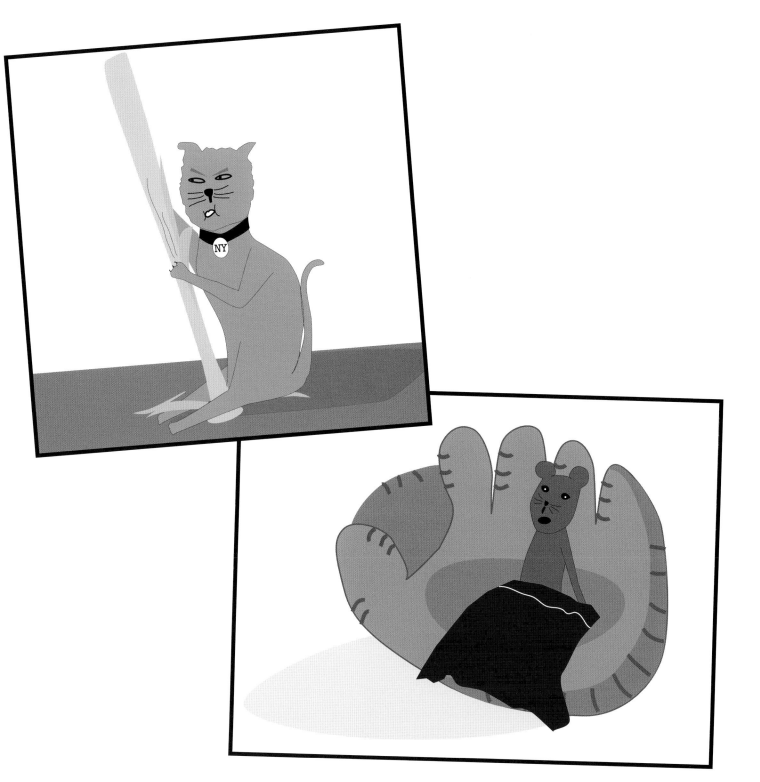

Slider, however, was hard at work in the Red Sox clubhouse. He had sharpened his nails to a fine point and was busy clawing the handles of each and every bat. "I'm so clever," Slider thought. "This plan worked wonders today. The bat snapped in two on almost every swing. Tomorrow the Red Sox are in for even more trouble!"

Frankie tossed and turned. Sleep wasn't coming easily. "What is that noise?" he thought impatiently. Irritated, Frankie threw back the covers and went to find out where the sound was coming from.

The Plan Continues

The noise grew louder as Frankie walked down the hall. He peeked into the clubhouse and found a cloud of sawdust. Slider was in the middle of it, scratching away. Frankie was shocked.

"No wonder the bats were breaking!" he gasped as he scurried in to get a better look. Slider was so wrapped up in his job, he didn't notice the spying mouse.

Then the door flew wide open. It was the Cardinal, Oriole, and the Blue Jay.

"How's it going, Boss?"

Frankie couldn't believe his eyes. "What could three birds want with a cat?"

"I'm just finishing up here," Slider said, licking his paws clean. "How did it go with the baseballs? Did you loosen all the strings?"

"All done!" boasted the Blue Jay.

"I can't wait to see how they hit them," laughed the Cardinal. "Those Sox don't stand a chance!"

Interrupting them, Slider growled, "Time's-a-wasting. Help me clean up this mess, and then get going on the next task."

Frankie pieced the information together. It seemed that ever since the cat arrived, the Red Sox were on a losing streak. "First the cat stole the pitcher's good luck charm. Then he and his pals rigged the bats and the balls. They're sabotaging the Red Sox! I have to stop them, but how?"

With a flurry of flapping, the birds left the clubhouse, and Frankie followed. "I have to save the Red Sox!" he thought.

He scampered through the concourse as fast as his legs could carry him. The birds were quick, but Frankie was determined. Once in a while, the birds swooped down to collect things. One dipped down for some leaves, another for twigs, and the third for cotton candy. Frankie wasn't sure what they were up to, but he kept up his pace.

The birds made a beeline for the room with the organ. "What are they doing in there?" Frankie wondered. He slipped inside to get a better look just as the Oriole fluttered out of an organ pipe. The cotton candy that the bird carried earlier was no longer in his beak. There was a clatter, and Frankie realized the other birds were flitting about inside the organ, purposely clogging its pipes.

"Hey, Jay, play a key—let's test this out!" crowed the Cardinal.

"Okay, hold on to your feathers!" called the Blue Jay.

The Jay threw all of his weight down on two keys, and the organ choked out a "*GHHHHULLLLLUGGGG*."

"Heeheehee," the birds twittered. "That sounded pathetic!"

Frankie thought back to yesterday's game. "No wonder the crowd wasn't charged up when the organ was playing!"

After the birds had a good laugh, they were off again. This time Frankie stayed put. There was a lot to do. First he had to clear out these pipes, but he would need some help. Legs was just the friend to ask. His many hands made light work.

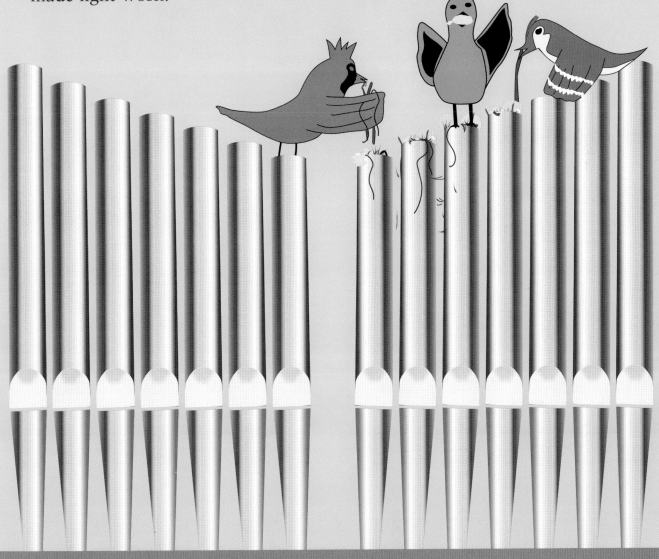